Jax Plays
Hide & Seek

Written By Veronica Cameron
Illustrated by Danh Tran Art

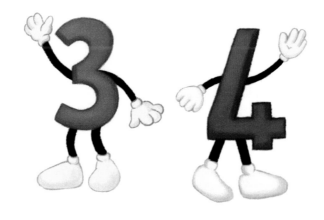

This book belongs to...
....

THE COOL REEDS®

FOR ZACHARY & XAVIER
YOU CAN ALWAYS COUNT ON ME

Jax Plays
Hide & Seek

I'm playing
hide and seek
with friends.
The fun with them
it never ends!

Jax looks
down
and sees a shoe.
Can you spot the
number 2?

Jax peaks through the bedroom door. Can you spot the number 4?

Jax looks by the big beehive. Can you spot the number 5?

Jax walks by
the pile of sticks.
Can you spot
the number 6?

Jax hears
giggles
from the heavens
Can you spot
the number 7?

Jax sees
movement
by the gate.
Can you spot
the number 8?

Jax looks out
to read the sign.
Can you spot
the number 9?

Jax must find
just one more
friend.
Can you spot
the number 10??

One, Two,
Three
Four, Five, Six
Seven, Eight
Nine and Ten.
The End!

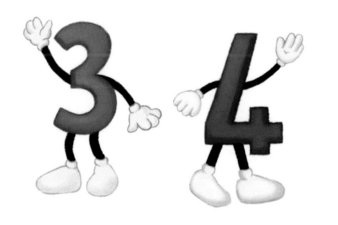

THE COOL REEDS®

A message from Veronica Cameron, creator of The Cool Reeds:

"Thank you for reading and supporting us!
Please head over to thecoolreeds.com
using code "friendofjax" for 10% off any item.

Follow us on Instagram, Facebook and Twitter
at thecoolreeds for more updates.
Adventure Awaits!
xoxo, Veronica"

Turn to the next couple of pages
for a free gift!

Jax Plays
Hide & Seek
COLORING BOOK

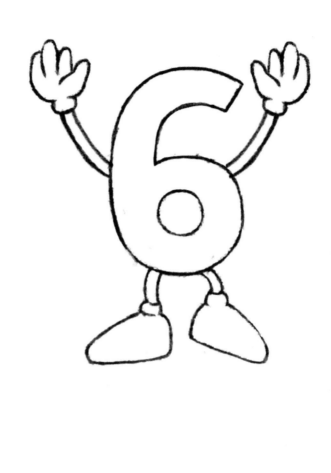

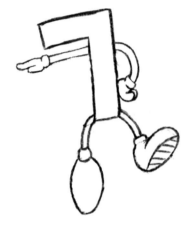

Made in the USA
Lexington, KY
21 December 2019